MY PET HUMAN

Yasmine Surovec

ROARING BROOK PRESS
New York

To Alex, Victor, Puppy, and our cats

Copyright © 2015 by Yasmine Surovec
Published by Roaring Brook Press
Roaring Brook Press is a division of Holtzbrinck Publishing Holdings Limited Partnership
175 Fifth Avenue, New York, New York 10010
mackids.com

Library of Congress Cataloging-in-Publication Data
Surovec, Yasmine, author, illustrator.
 My pet human / Yasmine Surovec. — First edition.
  pages cm
 Summary: A cat that enjoys his carefree life gets some treats and backrubs from the humans
who have just moved into his favorite abandoned house, then sets out to train them properly, all
the while protesting to his friends that he has no interest in being tied down to a human pet.
 ISBN 978-1-62672-073-2 (hardback)
 [1. Cats—Fiction.]   I. Title
 PZ7.S965626My 2015
 [Fic]—dc23

                                                              2014042460

Roaring Brook Press books may be purchased for business or promotional use.
For information on bulk purchases please contact Macmillan Corporate and Premium
Sales Department at (800) 221-7945 x5442 or by email at specialmarkets@macmillan.com.

First edition 2015
Book design by Roberta Pressel
Printed in the United States of America by R. R. Donnelley & Sons Company, Crawfordsville, Indiana
10 9 8 7 6 5 4 3 2 1

CONTENTS

CHAPTER 1
Mr. Independent

GEORGE'S
APARTMENT

FARRAH'S HOUSE

BEN'S HOUSE

I'm a lucky cat. I live a carefree life.

This is my territory. I know these streets like the back of my paw. Lots of cats are tied down by staying with their pet humans, but not me. I'm my own cat, and the only one I have to look out for is myself. I wouldn't have it any other way.

All I have to do is follow a few rules to stay on easy street.

DOWNTOWN

THE TWIRLING FORK

SUPERMARKET WITH FREE SAMPLES

AWESOME CHINESE FOOD

First, know the good places in town to eat. The supermarket has free samples, and the dumpster at the Chinese restaurant is full of leftovers too.

But the Twirling Fork is the best place to find grub: spaghetti and meatballs, pizza, roasted chicken . . . all the good stuff!

I just wait at the back of the restaurant until I see someone take a break. It's usually one of the cooks or waiters.

Once he sees me, I give him "the Look."

It took me a while to master "the Look," but it's essential to getting what I want from humans. And let's just say, I always get what I want. I mean, who can resist this face? I'm adorable!

"The Look" doesn't seem to work on all humans.

See that truck right there patrolling the neighborhood? That's bad news right there. The man inside rides around town looking for cats and dogs. He traps them in little cages and takes them to the pound!

I've heard that in the pound, hundreds of cats and dogs in cages are crying and howling to get out.

I've never been there but I'd rather not find out the hard way if it's true. That's why the #1 rule of the street is STAY ALERT!

This leads to the next rule: always have a good hiding spot.

I like the tree across from the empty house on the corner. No one has lived there for ages. The tree is perfect for a cat like me.

My last rule for a happy, carefree life is to have a few trusty friends. This yellow house is my friend Ben's place. It's really big and fancy.

And this is Ben, aka Mr. Fluffypuffypaws. He's got a lot of pet humans.

He has to deal with them every day. Or until they go to bed. IF they go to bed.

In Ben's backyard is a sweet doghouse where Ben hangs out to get away from it all. It's also where I usually meet up with him and a couple of other friends.

Farrah lives with her pet human in that white glass box on top of the hill.

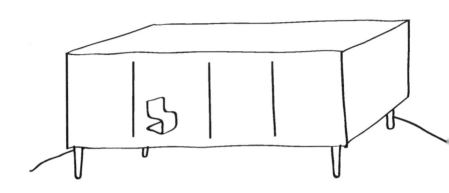

Her human spoils her and gives her whatever she wants.

And this is George. George lives with a little boy and his dad in a small apartment on the other side of town.

But unlike Ben's crazy kids, George's pet human is extremely quiet and shy. He's so shy that he locks himself in his bedroom most days to play video games.

Sometimes, my friends ask me why I don't get my own pet human. They just don't know how hard it would be to find one right for me!

My pet human would have to be perfect! He or she MUST:

1) Feed me LOTS of treats

2) Give me back rubs

SCRITCH
SCRITCH

3) Have plenty of boxes for me to play with

4) Be lots of fun

5) NOT smoosh me on the face, squeeze me too tightly, or pull my whiskers and tail

6) Let me sleep on his or her lap

7) Feed me a LOT!

8) Be a good and faithful companion

The perfect human just doesn't exist. They're crazy, aloof, moody, or high maintenace. I don't want to deal with that.

My friends just don't understand. I like living alone.

When they go back to their humans for the night, there's plenty I can do myself.

I can go to the Twirling Fork. I can find a tree to sleep in. I can—

Wait, where did he come from? Run!

Phew! I lost him. I have to be careful. No one is looking out for me except me.

I've had some close calls with the law, but I make sure I never get caught.

PHEW! WITH MY AMAZING AGILITY AND SPEED, I WAS ABLE TO OUTRUN HIM!

Sure, there are some benefits to having a pet human, like animal control would leave me alone. But no human can pin me down. I love my freedom way too much. I'm better off on my own.

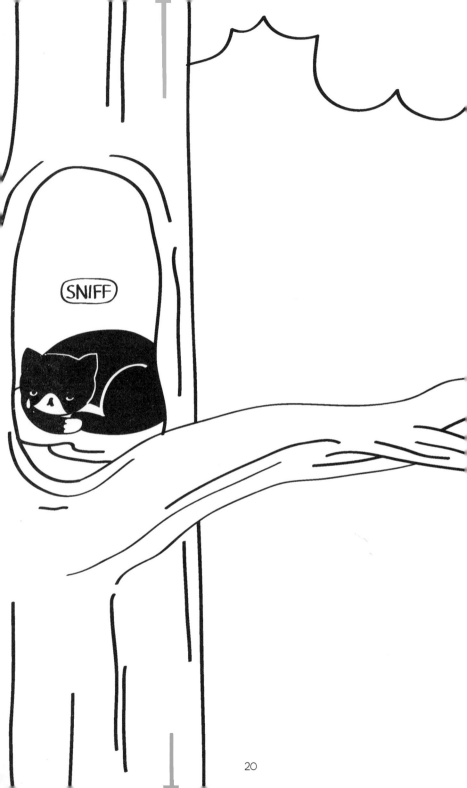

CHAPTER 2
Lost and Found

People are moving into the abandoned house. Maybe I should investigate.

I smell something awesome. My nose is telling me that the scent is coming from that house. I missed dinner last night and I'm starving!

Hm, I see a little human girl . . . with a bowl of macaroni and cheese topped with TUNA! I must get my paws on that!

This is a challenge. Little humans tend to be a bit nutty.

But it's nothing I can't handle. Watch a master at work.

I pop in the window and settle by her feet.

Major charm is the trick to getting what I want.

Remember "the Look" I talked about earlier? It's time to unleash it.

The weepy, doe-eyed look gets me what I want almost every time.

It's kind of weird being ogled at while I'm eating, but I'm so hungry, I'll ignore her.

IF YOU'RE STILL A BIT HUNGRY, THERE'S ONE LAST CAN OF TUNA IN THE CUPBOARD.

OH, AND HERE, TRY SOME OLIVES. WE HAVE LOTS!

AFTERWARD, I HAVE A BOX FOR YOU TO PLAY WITH!

I'VE ALWAYS WANTED A KITTY!

I WONDER WHAT AN OLIVE IS.

HM! TASTY!

An older human comes into the room. Unlike the little human, she's a little bit more, um, unfriendly. But that's okay. I'll just gobble up this bowl of food and then I'm outta here.

ACK! WHY IS THAT STRAY CAT IN THE HOUSE?

AW, MOM! DON'T SCARE HIM AWAY!

ISN'T HE CUTE?

I think it's time to go! I pretty much just stuck around for the grub.

Tuna? Olives? If she insists!

I don't think they understand that I'm not hanging around much longer. I just stopped by for tuna . . .

. . . and this thing, whatever it is.

CAT FOUND

IS THIS YOUR KITTY?

FOUND ON CENTRAL AND 3RD.

HE'S A TUXEDO CAT AND HE LOVES TO EAT!

IF HE IS YOURS, CALL 555-8642.

She definitely doesn't understand that I'm not staying or that no one's looking for me. In the meantime, I'll stick around and play with these boxes.

NOPE! This is not my idea of a good time!

Ick. I hate getting wet! Yeesh! Baths are the worst!

Humans and their baths . . . I don't get it. This is not how I clean myself!

But I like these cozy boxes. I'll probably have time for a little cat nap before I go.

CHAPTER 3
How to Train a Human

This human thinks that she can bribe me into staying forever with food.

And back rubs! Hmm . . . some humans aren't as annoying as I'd thought.

Oh look, my friends are here!

Hi, Ben! Hi, Farrah! Hi, George!

Staying at the humans' house has been a blast, and it's not as bad as I'd imagined it would be. But I was glad to see my friends.

Ben and Farrah and George had lots of questions for me. They were kinda surprised that I was hanging out with some humans.

YEAH, BUT THESE HUMANS AREN'T CRAZY. THE LITTLE HUMAN I MET DOESN'T SMOTHER ME TO PIECES.

But I told them about the boxes...

and the back scratches...

and most importantly, the bowls of olives and tuna and mac 'n' cheese!

They still didn't get it.

Hm. Now I don't know what to do. Part of me is thinking that I shouldn't stay too long and warm up to these humans. I mean, I'm my own cat, and I don't need to be responsible for a pet human! But another part of me is saying this is a pretty sweet set-up.

Going about town looking for food can be tiring. Sure, humans are unpredictable, but what if . . . I can train them? Now training a human to feed me all the treats that I want, I can see that happening.

I don't take off. I go inside instead.

I can definitely train this little human to be my pet. She already adores me.

How difficult can it be to give me treats on demand?

First, I try purring.

When that doesn't work, I try meowing. A lot.

Sometimes humans are kinda slow to get things.

When all else fails, I give her "the Look."

See? It works! And to reward her, I give her a head boop to show my appreciation.

And that is how to train a human. Persistence.
Patience. And rewards for good behavior.

It's just that simple.

Now, if I'm going to stay here, I also need to train the mother human. While the little human is easy to train, the mom is a bit more . . . challenging. Older humans tend to be set in their ways.

PLEASE PUT THAT BOX AWAY.

She's no fun at all.

DON'T FEED HIM TOO MUCH, OR HE'LL GET FAT!

She tends to bark orders.

And she gets annoyed easily.

But I can change all that! With a little time and patience, I can get any human to warm up. How? It's the simple gestures that make a big difference.

For example, I know the mother human likes it when I swish my tail against her face, especially when she's trying to read or getting ready for bed.

All humans like presents. I give her a present from my daily adventures as an expert domestic hunter. Humans, after all, make horrible hunters.

My most favorite animals to hunt are vicious snakes caught in the wild, like underneath the flower pot in the backyard.

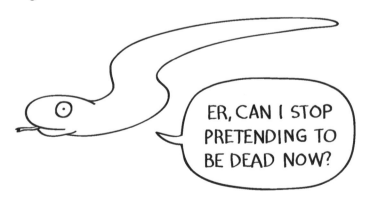

I can tell she's excited by my present!

Or maybe not. Some humans are hard to please.

Lastly, remember how a cat's belly is irresistible to humans?

I've been told that my belly is soft as a fluffy cloud. No one can resist my magical belly. Not even grumpy humans.

See? It's easy to get humans to warm up. Like I said, it just takes a little time, a little effort, and a lot of smarts (which is something I have tons of).

In no time, I'll have these pet humans wrapped around my furry little paws. I've been staying here for several days, and I gotta admit, life has been good. I've got toys and treats and tuna and olives, and I don't even have to go scrounging around town to find them!

But of course my friends come over and check up on me. And they have a thing or two to say. "It's not always about you," Ben tells me.

But I don't have a pet human. I'm just hanging out here for a while until I figure out what I want to do. In the meantime, I have a little human I've trained to give me what I want.

I guess I'll get more tuna and olives and back scratches if the humans under my training are A-OK. It's just that as I've mentioned before, humans tend to be a bit moody.

CHAPTER 4
Operation Find-a-Friend

Lately, all the little human does is sulk.

I have to fix her. Maybe my irresistible charm will do the trick!

I try purring loudly and rolling on the floor to show how cute I am. After all, the little human likes cute things.

I lend her my favorite toys.

I've been told that I have a beautiful voice, so I sing her a song.

I show her this funny-looking spider I found hanging on the window sill.

I mean, he's funny-looking!

I even bring her THIS AWESOME BOX! Who doesn't love a good ol' box?

I guess she doesn't.

When I'm feeling down, I go see Ben, Farrah, and George. They're good friends. They are always there for me.

Little human should have friends just like I do. Then she wouldn't be so sad.

They could play in boxes.

Look for bugs in the grass.

And eat tuna fish sandwiches with olives!

That's my new plan. It isn't going to be easy, but I'm going to help her make a new friend!

I would ask Ben. He's got a whole bunch of little humans—maybe they could be her friends. But they're on vacation.

I'll ask Farrah. She's not usually around little humans, but she might have a helpful suggestion.

TRY ASKING GEORGE. HE'S GOT A LITTLE HUMAN SHE COULD BE FRIENDS WITH, BUT IT MAY TAKE A BIT MORE WORK SINCE HIS HUMAN USUALLY KEEPS TO HIMSELF.

George likes my idea to get his human and my human to hang out. So we come up with an elaborate plan, which involves a lot of wit and cunning, something George and myself both have tons of.

Now let Operation Find-a-Friend begin!
I need something of value, something to use as bait.

I know exactly what to use.

This should lure her out of the house.

WHERE ARE YOU GOING WITH MY HAT?

Now that I've got her outside, I need to make sure she's headed toward George's apartment. Hopefully George has stuck to the plan.

George's job was to lure his little human outside, which I'm sure wasn't easy. His human hardly ever leaves the house.

I throw my human's hat into the bush too. That's the last part of the plan.

See, the way Operation Find-a-Friend works is, you take two shy kids out of their comfort zones, and, somehow, get them to meet up. It's a bit tricky, really.

But we can always hope that it works!

And it did! Look at their happy faces.

And now a beautiful friendship begins, I hope.

George and I couldn't believe it. His human is … talking. They're having an actual conversation!

There's nothing more satisfying than executing a plan perfectly! We actually got our humans to become friends.

They're going inside George's building. I think they are going to read comic books.

Things worked out really well. I knew it would! I mean, I never doubted for a second.

But wait a minute. My human is gone.

Really, what do I care? My job here is done. My friends are happy. The little humans are happy.

Time for me to move along, I suppose.

CHAPTER 5
My Pet Human

My human hasn't even come out to look for me. I guess she found a new friend. She doesn't need me anymore.

I think of the tuna. I think of the olives. I think of the boxes. I think of my little human. It was just too good to be true.

I guess I'm off . . . I shouldn't be too sad. I'm a cat!

Good thing I don't have a pet human to worry about! If no one has time for me, then I don't have time for them. So off I go!

Look out world, here I come!

I remember our good times together. I remember our head boop.

Oh well. Since I'm back on my own, I can't forget the first rule of the street: stay alert!

Oh no! Animal Control!
I zig. I zag.
But I can't avoid the net.

THIS
CAN'T
BE
HAPPENING!!!

THIS IS HORRIBLE! I've had nightmares about this, and it never ends well.

Wh-what's going to happen to me?!
I can almost hear the cries from the pound already.

This is not how I wanted things to end! I want to go home! I want my friends! I wanna get outta here!

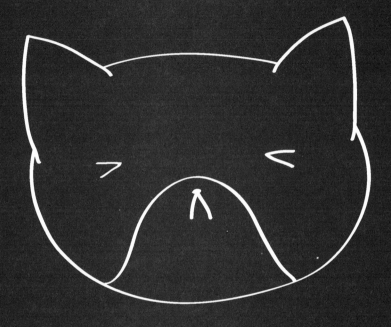

I'M GONNA DIE ALONE!!!

Wait . . . I hear someone outside the truck.

I hear yelling. I hear the little human's voice.

Is she here to get me out? Please save me! I can't spend the rest of my life in cat jail. PLEASE!

No, don't listen to anything Animal Control has to say!

I hear another voice. It sounds familiar. Is it . . . little human's MOTHER?

I thought she HATED me. Wow, she sure did a good job playing hard to get. Now please! Get me outta this place!

And the moment I heard the click, I just knew.

I had my pet human.

And she is perfect in every way.

It's not just my little human and my big human there either. It's all my friends! Ben, Farrah, George, and George's pet human, Liam. They all came to save me!

HEY! YOU SHOULD COME OVER TO OUR HOUSE TOMORROW.

I GUESS IT'S TIME TO TAKE DOWN THOSE "MISSING CAT" SIGNS.

WE HAVE AN INFLATABLE POOL IN OUR BACKYARD!

OKAY, I'LL BRING MY GOGGLES.

My pet human hugs me tight and carries me home.

She wants to give me a name. Little human isn't very good with names. While she thinks about it, I've already decided what to call her. She looks like a Freckles to me. Because, you know, she has freckles. So I'll be calling her that.

She thinks about names for a long time. While she's rubbing my belly. While she's washing dishes . . .

While she's feeding me tuna and olives . . .

And then finally she gets it right.

The End